Rissa's secret weapon

More Books from Macy & JC

TALES OF A TEENAGE ALIEN HUMAN HYBRID
The Alien's Daughter
The Hybrid Challenge

COMING SOON
The Human Complication

SILVER CITY PRINCESSES
Cindy's Demanding Day
A challenge for Maree
Rissa's Secret Weapon

COMING SOON
Isabelle and the Beastly Bookworm

Rissa's Secret Weapon

SILVER CITY PRINCESS STORIES

BOOK THREE

MACY MORROWS

JC MORROWS

S&G PUBLISHING

For the little girl who somehow survived twelve years in school surrounded by people doing all they could to destroy her... shatter her... rob her of the smallest amount of joy.
You. Did. Not. Let. Them. Win!

*Play your fight song **loud**, girl!*

"The quickest WAY TO ACQUIRE self-confidence is to do EXACTLY what you are afraid to do"

– unknown

Rissa dropped a pinch of salt into the large mixing bowl, and then stirred it slowly into the other ingredients.

This was one of her favorite things

about being in the kitchen—putting everything together. She never tired of finding new ways to make things, experimenting with recipes, and adding ingredients no one would ever expect.

She took great pleasure in surprising those who tasted her finished meals. If someone expected the same old familiar taste in anything she made, they were always in for a surprise—usually one they greatly enjoyed.

Rissa knew some people thought she was a bit too proud of her creations, but cooking was the one thing in her life that she never questioned.

She knew she was an exceptional cook. . . gifted even. But she never considered herself overly proud. The fact that people enjoyed her creations just added to the fun of cooking.

If only every area of life were so simple...

There were no other parts of Rissa's life that were as easy, as natural for her, as exceptional, as cooking.

Of course, if she had to choose one area over every other, she would pick the kitchen.

Every time she came home with a note from her teacher about another incident of bullying, Rissa used it to try to convince her mother that she should be schooled at home.

And every time her mother pointed

out that being home-schooled would make it far too easy for Rissa to lock herself away in the kitchen all the time.

To which Rissa would argue that her culinary education was too important to spend too much time away from the kitchen.

And then her mother would point out how important it was for a chef to know how to deal with people. It was not something she could learn being tucked away from them all. Which was why, in the end, her mother always won.

And so Rissa attended Silver City Preparatory Academy, where she consoled herself with being a top chef.

Mom had also told her more times

than she could count that the other kids teased her the most because they were jealous of her talent—not that it ever felt that way to her.

When they walked by her at lunch, making mooing sounds. . . when they commented that it was a good thing everyone could tell how much she enjoyed her own food. . . when they joked that the door to the cooking lab would need to be widened after another year or two of her taking classes. . . it felt a lot less like jealousy than plain old-fashioned meanness.

But she had tired of arguing with her mom about it, so she refused to bring it up again unless her teacher sent a note home about it.

Just then, behind her a timer dinged, and she turned to pull out the bottom crusts for the pot pies she had decided to make for dinner.

As she turned back, she caught her reflection in the shiny toaster. For the life of her, she couldn't figure out where half the hateful jabs came from. Sure, she wasn't especially tall, and no part of her was skinny, but her doctor had never said anything about her being overweight.

If she was, wouldn't her pediatrician have said something by now, especially with more than half the country struggling with obesity.

"Rissa, sweet pea, that smells heavenly." Dad's deep voice held a note of appreciation that always touched Rissa.

He walked over to where she was stirring together the ingredients for the pot pie, looking over her shoulder.

"You sure do make it hard to wait for dinner, sweet pea." The twinkle in his eye and the playful tone of his voice told her he was just teasing, which warmed her heart.

Teasing—like Dad did—never bothered her. He loved her. She never questioned that. And his teasing was never mean. Mostly it was his way of complimenting her without being obvious about it, like complaining that he had to wait for dinner.

If only my schoolmates would take lessons from him. . .

She shook off the dark mood that was attempting to settle over her.

There was nothing she could do about her classmates, except love them and pray for them, like her mom told her. . . and then ignore them, like her dad told her.

Chapter Two

Navigating the

lunch-room was one of Rissa's least favorite parts of the school day. If she had her way, she would eat outside every day, rain or shine. But when the weather was rainy or cold, the doors that led to a small cluster of outdoor tables—and the grassy hill where she usually sat—were closed and locked.

For the safety of the students. Indeed. Oh, if only they knew...

Sitting on the far side of the grassy hill, out of sight of her fellow students was the only place she felt safe eating.

The whispers she could ignore all together. After all, she didn't actually *know* they were talking about her. She usually missed most of the looks because she'd learned long ago it was better not to look at the other students as she walked by with her food.

It was the laughter that started just as she passed by, and the comments spoken just loudly enough for her to hear, but not loud enough to be heard by the teachers.

Where do school kids learn to be so mean?

Her classmates certainly didn't use much cleverness when it came to cooking. It made her feel a little better about the teasing to know that not only could she out-cook anyone in the room, but since she brought her own creations, it was a pretty safe assumption that she would enjoy her lunch more than anyone else, too.

She breathed a little easier when she reached the far side of the room, where there were several empty tables.

She could sit alone and have an

empty table between her and the rest of the teens and pre-teens in the room.

She slid onto a seat that faced the windows overlooking their outdoor eating area, longing for the quiet spot where she usually ate in peace.

It had rained most of the morning, but the sun was beginning to peek through the clouds, and the sight of the wet pavement sparkling in the sudden shafts of light was a peaceful enough view to relax her enough to enjoy her meal.

After lunch was advanced cooking techniques, a class with only a dozen students. Sadly, Poppy—her least favorite student in the whole school—was one of them.

Rissa walked in with a smile, moving immediately to her station so she could begin setting up.

Their instructor had already put several instructions on the board at the front of class and Rissa could hardly wait to get started. She followed the instructions as far as she could, and then waited for her classmates to settle down so the class would get started.

"Hmm." The comment came from behind her, and Rissa resisted the urge to turn around, even when the next words were spoken. "Always in a hurry when it comes to food, aren't you."

The voice could only belong to Poppy. And while it might be a mystery to Rissa how someone with such a sweet name could be such a jerk, her flowery name certainly didn't hold her back one bit.

Rissa rearranged utensils that really didn't need rearranging, she straightened her supplies, and then she sat as still as she could, determined to ignore the baiting of her classmate.

"Is it just the love of food that makes you want to be a cook, Rissa?" Her voice was getting louder now. Several students around them had stopped talking, and were listening intently.

The urge to turn around was stronger

now. For too long, Poppy had gotten away with being nasty.

If only I knew what to say back to her.

Somehow, whenever Rissa tried to make a comment back to Poppy, it either made things worse or got her into trouble.

"What? No one ever told you white is a bad color for people who are…"

Rissa gritted her teeth together while Poppy searched for the worst word she could think of.

"…wide, shall we say?"

Rissa felt her mouth open, felt a fiery jerk of shock to her system, a snap as her jaws separated quickly, a sudden, stabbing pain in her chest area as the breath she struggled to pull in fought to reach her lungs, but no words came to her.

No thoughts registered in her brain.

Even her emotions felt as if they had been shaken up, swished around and then spewed out.

Poppy's voice had risen so much with her final words that it was as loud as the noise level of the rest of the room.

Several students who had been walking back to their stations were now stopped in front of Rissa, their faces clearly visible to her as they stood only a few feet in front of the table where she had been gathering ingredients and supplies of her own.

Several of them were laughing, but at

least two girls were wearing nearly identical masks of shock and horror, and one boy looked almost as if someone had punched him in the stomach unexpectedly.

From somewhere behind her, there was the sound of laughter.

In the distance, a bell rang.

The sound of hard-soled shoes, like the clogs their instructor was fond of, sounded on the floor.

Then someone was talking, telling students to get to their stations, reciting instructions.

The students, the bell, the shoes, the voice—they all registered vaguely in Rissa's mind, but nothing managed to block out the agony that was ripping through her from the ugly words. Nothing in sight took away the haze that told Rissa she was close to tears.

And she was still fighting for breath, as if Poppy's words had somehow thickened the air in the room around them.

The only thing that stood out was the knowledge that once again Poppy, a girl she had known for ten years, someone who had grown up in a house down the street from her, who had ridden her bike alongside Rissa too many times to count, who had been in the same class with her through the years, had spoken loudly enough for everyone in the room to hear.

It was like a monster, throwing a

verbal punch that was designed to rob Rissa of air and sight and balance, and then laughed over it, as if she had not just verbally stabbed her classmate—someone she had once called friend—in the back.

"Rissa!" The volume of the voice calling her name and the feel of someone shaking her managed to pull a fraction of her attention away from the pain in her chest.

She looked up to see who had shouted—and met the concerned expression of her teacher.

"Rissa, are you sick? Do you need to go see the school nurse?"

The nurse? What could the school nurse do to help me?

There was no cure for the pain Rissa was feeling, no pill that would make the agony disappear, no treatment that would take away the scars that would forever mark her—down to her very soul.

"Rissa, you cannot be sick in here. You need to go to the nurse. Alex, come help."

A moment later, strong hands were pulling at her—the teacher—and someone else.

She didn't resist. She simply followed along, moving slowly and stumbling over her own feet along the way.

Chapter Three

There was a loud sound behind her, a strong gust of wind, and then silence. The hands still pulled at her.

She took a few steps, then stopped,

unable to go on. After a few seconds of struggling to pull away from the hands that were still trying to pull her down the hall, she stopped fighting and simply slumped to the floor, leaning heavily against the wall that, thankfully, slowed her descent and kept her from falling over into a heap on the floor.

Everything that had been fuzzy was beginning to lose focus, and some instinct deep within her must have taken over as her brain began to simply shut down.

Her head dropped and somehow the air began to flow a bit easier. The stabbing pain in her chest eased just enough that she was able to take slightly larger breaths. The fuzzy haze retreated around the edges of her vision and the world started to come back into focus.

"Hey, you're not gonna pass out, are you?"

She didn't answer.

She sat there, just as she was, propped against the wall, as she forced each breath in and then out, closing her eyes and opening them again after a few seconds, forcing herself to think of nothing but breathing, almost desperate now to calm her stampeding heartbeat.

"Do I need to go get someone?"

She said nothing.

Time passed silently. Somewhere in the distance a door shut loudly.

She breathed.

"Rissa, come on now. Say something.

Do something. Give me some sign you're still with me. I don't know what to do here."

When he said her name, his voice was filled with fear and uncertainty. Not the kind that comes from being afraid you've done something that has hurt a person, but the kind that says you're genuinely worried that someone you care for is hurt.

Something happened within Rissa. Her chest constricted again, but not from pain. Her breath came quicker. Her heart beat erratically.

It was unfamiliar. . . foreign enough to finally distract her from the feelings that had consumed her only moments ago.

Someone cared. . . for her. Worried

over her. . . wanted to help her.

It was a revelation.

She looked up.

The boy who looked back down at her was familiar, but she couldn't remember his name.

She had probably seen him in class every day, but there was not a single time she could think of when he had spoken to her, not once that someone had said his name where she could hear. When she tried to think back to what her teacher had said just before they had pulled her from the classroom, her chest tightened again in a painful way.

"Come on, now. Don't do that again. You were doing better just a few seconds ago." His voice was filled with concern and, again, it distracted her enough to throw her off balance and calm the emotional upheaval that was trying to wreck her.

"Yeah. That's it. Just breathe." He let out a hard exhale. "Please just don't pass out on me."

His voice almost made her want to laugh. The way he said "pass out" like he couldn't stand to say the word faint, or think about having to deal with her if she did happen to faint.

And suddenly, somehow, she was laughing. The picture in her mind, of him trying to drag her along behind him, all the way to the nurse's office was entirely too comical.

"And. . . now you're scaring me."

She looked up at him again. She didn't tell him how funny his face was. It really should not have been funny, but it was.

His expression was somewhere between terror and annoyance, one foot planted firmly, the other pointing out at an odd angle, his weight toward the front, like he was ready to run away if he had to.

But where would he go? To the nurse's office? Back to the classroom?

"Are you cracking up? Is that what's going on here?"

A short, bark of laughter escaped before Rissa could put a stop to it. He really thought she was crazy?

Like that could explain all of this…

On second thought, though…

Maybe she was a little crazy. Maybe that was why this particular situation was funny to her. Perhaps it was why she found herself laughing when she had been struggling to breathe just minutes ago.

Maybe I should just get off the floor and make my way to the nurse's office.

At least that way she wouldn't have to go back to class. . . not yet, anyway.

Chapter Four

Fortunately the school nurse was well acquainted with Rissa's many strange health conditions, so no questions where asked when she showed up in her office, pale and leaning heavily on her classmate, whose name she still had not managed to remember.

He moved toward a paper-covered table that was pushed up against one wall of the small office, until the nurse stopped him, gesturing instead to a couch placed against another wall.

"Panic attack?"

Rissa nodded.

There was a strange sound from beside her that she wondered at.

The boy supported her weight as they crossed the room, then he helped her settle onto the couch. The nurse handed him a note and before Rissa had a chance to thank him or ask him his name, the nurse had ushered him out into the hall.

She let her head drop onto the plush arm of the sofa. It had been a very confusing day, and her thoughts were still swirling all around in her head, making no sense.

Poppy had gotten the best of her. . . again.

That was the way these things always went. Especially lately. Poppy's arsenal of insults was obviously very well stocked, and Rissa's knowledge ran more to recipes than rude comments.

She could memorize a recipe after looking it through one time. Then she memorized her own variations of it. It should be something to be proud of. It was the sort of skill that most chefs aspired to.

It could have been a tremendous boon for her. Instead, it felt like a curse, that she couldn't somehow use it to throw verbal insults back at Poppy and the others who joined in with her, teasing Rissa and some of the other kids they attended school with.

If she couldn't find a way to turn off her own reactions to Poppy's words, the next best thing would be a comeback or two.

But no matter how she tried, she could not seem to come up with something she could say to bullies to make them back off.

"Poppy again?" There was no surprise in the nurse's voice, only an acceptance that made Rissa very very sad.

If even the school nurse could see there was a problem, why was it that none of the other adults could?

"Do you want me to call your mother or your father this time, Rissa?"

Rissa cringed. Her father was by far the best choice, but her mother had mentioned at least a dozen times in the last couple of days that he had a lot more to do that usual this week at work.

It shouldn't have been a struggle to decide...but it was.

She knew if she called her father, he would be less judgemental about the whole thing. She also knew that if she did call Dad, she would not hear the end of it from her mom for days.

His work at the lab was not only very

important to him, but his results helped so many people all over the world. If this was one of those times...

On the other hand, she would probably hear from Mom for days about having another *attack* at school.

Her mother did her work at home, in her own personal art studio. There were times Rissa wished. . . so much. . . that she would outgrow the studio and move into a larger one, away from home, but so far it hadn't happened.

She let out a sigh while she thought it over and the nurse noticed. "I would wonder why it's such a hard decision, but I know your mother pretty well."

She grinned, but there was no laughter or dismissal in her words—or her smile. In a lot of ways, Rissa felt just as responsible to Nurse Goodwyn as she did to herself.

The lady who had never been anything but wonderful to Rissa had unfortunately been on the receiving end of more than one rant from her mother in the past when she'd arrived to pick up her daughter and the nurse was the only person in view.

"Your dad?"

Rissa shook her head. She knew it was not the right choice, however tempting it was. "Crazy busy week at work."

"Your mom, then?"

"Do we have to?" Rissa knew she was whining a little, but she really did not want to deal with her mother.

"It was a panic attack, you're sure?" Mrs. Goodwyn was stalling. She knew it. Rissa knew it. And they both knew she could only do it for so long, but Rissa played along for a minute in an attempt to keep her mother away just a little longer.

"I think so. I mean, I don't know of anything else it could have been. Maybe you should pull out that big book with a million diagnoses in it. We could be wrong, and we wouldn't want that . .. right?"

Nurse Goodwyn laughed. "That's a good one, Rissa. I didn't think of that one."

"Can't I just go back to class?" And

before Mrs. Goodwyn could answer, she went on. "I mean, I could hang out here for another half hour and this class would be over, right?"

Nurse Goodwyn started to answer again, but Rissa rushed on. "If I miss the rest of this class, my stress level will have time to level out. Right?" Mrs. Goodwyn nodded slowly, clearly unsure where Rissa was going with her hypothetical thinking.

"Good. There's no Poppy in any of my other classes for the rest of the day. That should save me from a repeat." When Nurse Goodwyn nodded again, she kept going.

"So, if the reason behind my stress is eliminated for the rest of the day, I'll be fine in my other classes. Right?"

This time, Nurse Goodwyn spoke up before Rissa could interrupt again. "Yes, I suppose that is technically true, but you also know the doctor's orders as well as I do. After an attack, you are meant to rest."

When Rissa started to speak, she rushed on, putting special emphasis on the next words. "And you are not to put yourself into any stressful situations." She held up a hand when Rissa tried to interrupt again.

"No, now I know you don't see the reason for it, but I'm telling you right now, it's always better to follow the doctor's orders."

With a grin, she added, "After all, they

don't go to school forever just to know nothing, right?"

Rissa finally smiled at that, letting out a sigh only a moment later.

"Got it." She knew when she was beat. "Mom, I guess."

Nurse Goodwyn smiled, stood, and squeezed Rissa's shoulder as she walked past her on the way out.

"It's all going to be fine, dear. You'll see."

Chapter Five

Rissa's mother was not as understanding as Nurse Goodwyn had been, going on about Rissa allowing herself to be over-stimulated and taking things the wrong way as they drove toward home.

Rissa sat in the seat behind her mother, trying to make comments at the appropriate moments as she flipped through her social media feed on her phone.

She purposely did not follow any of her classmates, only pages that featured things like cooking, baking, and crafting.

It always helped to relax her after a panic attack, looking at what others had done with food—and it gave her ideas to try on her own.

"Clarissa, are you listening to me?"

"Yes, Mom. I am listening." She had been. She'd just taken a little too long to answer.

"What are you doing back there?" Since the SUV happened to be stopped at a traffic light, she turned in her seat, looking at her daughter in the back seat.

Rissa waved her phone, turning it around so her mother could see the screen. "It relaxes me."

"You really shouldn't be on social media, you know. Isn't that one of the things Dr. Pearson told you—that you should avoid things that are stressful for you."

Rissa shook her head just as her mother turned back to look forward again. "This isn't stressful for me. It's relaxing." A moment later she added, quietly enough—she hoped—that her mother wouldn't hear her, "I don't follow any of my classmates."

"Well, I want you to put it away when

we get home. You should rest. We don't want another trip to see Dr. Pearson so soon, do we?"

"You're right, Mom. I don't want that." What she didn't say was that her mother's comment was more stressful for her than the thought of looking at the social media stream of every single student she went to school with could ever have been.

Just like she didn't understand why the comments from her classmates hurt so much, her mom would never understand that her own comment felt more like a threat than concern.

Her lithe, willowy, graceful mother, who had likely never been even five pounds overweight in her life—and had the figure of a model—could never understand how it felt to be short and wider than many of the girls her age.

Having developed early, she had been taller than nearly everyone for almost two years. Then her body had started to curve and round out much earlier than every other girl in her class.

Now, everyone was starting to shoot past her in height. The other girls were all developing. . . and getting taller all at once.

Somehow, her height was stubbornly staying put. Or else she was moving upward at a snail's pace. The rest of her continued to curve and round, giving her an hourglass shape, but one that was much thicker all around than most of the other girls.

Rissa had been forced to accept some time ago that she might not get any taller at all. It was entirely possible she would take after her diminutive father. Not that he was freakishly short or anything—just that he was considerably shorter than Rissa's mother.

Well, not really. He was physically only an inch or so shorter. It was the stylish heels that her mother insisted on wearing that made such a difference when they were standing together.

When she thought about it, she realized her figure was more like his as well. He wasn't a heavyset man, just not at all skinny, which was no disaster for a man. For Rissa, however, it would be.

Just my luck.

The thought was only a little sour. She had decided long ago that she would rather have plain or homely looks than to be hateful and rude to people just to make herself feel better—or worse, just because she could.

When the SUV pulled into the large three-car garage, Rissa was out of her seat and out of the vehicle only seconds after her mother had turned the engine off.

She went through the door that

opened into the house, setting her cell phone in the charging station in the small room that connected the garage to the kitchen.

She picked up ingredients at random as she walked into and through the kitchen, setting them up on her counter.

She had nearly assembled everything for the panini she'd not gotten to make in class this afternoon, when her mother walked into the kitchen.

"Clarissa, this is not what I call resting."

She turned, having just pulled several things from the refrigerator. "I was just trying to finish what I didn't get to do in class."

"The class where you had your panic

attack?" There was something about her mother's voice that made Rissa very uncomfortable, but she wasn't quite sure what to make of it.

"Yes." She answered very carefully, keeping her tone as neutral as possible. "But it wasn't the assignment that caused a problem."

"Sweetheart, I know you enjoy cooking." She shook her head as she spoke. "I don't even pretend to know why."

Since her mother had never been much of a cook, her admission did not surprise Rissa in the least. However, she said nothing, waiting for her mother to make her point.

When she didn't, Rissa stood there for

several very heavy, tense moments before finally asking, "Is it bad that I enjoy cooking?"

Her mother answered quickly—a little too quickly. "No." She picked up the tomato Rissa had sat down just a minute ago, running a perfectly manicured nail over it.

"I just wonder if maybe your life would be a little easier if you stopped taking so many cooking-related classes at school."

Rissa opened her mouth to speak, but nothing came out. Her mother must have thought she was about to interrupt, because she quickly went on.

"Didn't you tell me that most of the incidents which cause your panic attacks have something to do with your weight?"

Rissa nodded slowly, still unable to think of what she could possibly say.

"Then don't you think it's possible that you would get a bit less teasing from your classmates if you stopped bringing your love of food to their attention?"

And still she had no words. She simply stood there, staring at her mother, the person who had made so little of the merciless teasing Rissa had received from her schoolmates for more years than she wanted to admit.

Was her mother really suggesting that it was a possibility that she would be teased less if she stopped cooking at school?

"I just want you to think about it, love. There are so many other classes we could transfer you into classes that are just as much fun as cooking." And with that, she swept out of the kitchen.

Rissa stood there, staring at the door her mother had just pushed through.

Her thoughts were a jumbled mess, and she was beginning to have difficulty breathing again.

There was a voice in her head that was nearly screaming! How could her mother not know how much it hurt to suddenly drop the bombshell that she'd been making light of all these years.

If she really thought her suggestion would help one bit with the torture

Rissa suffered daily at the hands of her peers, she was wrong.

Chapter Six

Rissa moved her shoulders and her hips, as she lip-synced to the song blasting through the wireless headphones that covered her ears.

It was the best thing she had discovered yet to help her deal with and move beyond the sort of nonsense she had to put up with from her classmates.

Fight song... Yes.

It was the perfect thing. It was definitely a fight to make herself go to school every day, to face the people who seemed to have made it their mission to make her miserable.

Fight was exactly what she needed to walk into school every day, to pass them in the hall, to see them snickering behind their hands—and still hold her head high.

Her head and shoulders moved back and forth as she bounced a little on the balls of her feet, her hands still stirring the ingredients slowly coming together in the large bowl she held.

She had finished the panini, and had taken half of one to her mother, grateful she'd said nothing more about her earlier comments.

Evidently, her mother had decided to put aside her argument temporarily, so Rissa had as well—at least for the moment.

Now she was making comfort food. The cook her mother had hired was making dinner in the main kitchen, so she'd moved to the smaller one in the pool house, the one with ingredients her mother did not approve of having in the main house except on special occasions.

And even though Rissa's favorite

maid kept the pool house kitchen stocked for her, brownies were still a rare treat. She didn't make them very often.

Despite what her classmates thought, she did not sit around and eat junk at home all the time. She mixed up a sweet treat no more than once a week.

They didn't even have dessert more than once a week—and it was usually something brought in from a bakery, even though Rissa had told her mother repeatedly that she enjoyed baking just as much as cooking.

When the song ended, she set down the bowl, let out a sigh and pulled the headphones from her head.

For a few minutes she had been able

to let go of everything that had happened, but thoughts of her mother—and her tormenters from school—continued to plague her.

She considered going for a swim, but being alone in the pool was not likely to be any better for her than being alone in the kitchen.

The real problem was that wherever she went, she would be alone with her thoughts, and music—even great music—could only distract her so much.

With her headphones off, the beep of her cell phone caught her attention and she reluctantly walked around the counter and over to the table where she had put down her phone earlier.

Her mother had said earlier that she

needed to spend less time on her phone, but she'd been quick to tell Rissa to take it with her when she headed for the pool house.

When she picked up the slim phone, she could see she had a text message by the little bubble notification that lit up her screen.

"Hey, Rissa. Hope this is cool. N...

This was all she could see until she swiped at the notification to open it.

When the whole thing popped up, she read over it again, curious as to who could be texting her out of the blue.

"Hey, Rissa. Hope this is cool. Nurse Goodwyn gave me your number when I went by to check on you between classes."

There was no name, just a string of numbers at the top. Just then the phone vibrated in her hand as another text appeared.

"This is the first chance I've had to text again. Homework, you know. . . How are you?"

Rissa stood there holding the phone for what felt like forever before finally typing back.

"I'm fine. Who is this?"

There was no way she was admitting to anything other than fine, just in case it happened to be Poppy or one of her friends.

Another message quickly popped up.

"Oops. Sorry. It's Alex. You know. . . from school. I helped you to the nurse's

office this afternoon."

Rissa laughed. She couldn't help herself. How badly did he think a panic attack affected her?

Well, maybe it's not so silly. It did send me home for the rest of the day after all.

She thought for a second before typing back. *"I got it. Thanks for that, BTW."*

A second after she typed her words and hit SEND, the phone vibrated again.

"Sucks you had to go home. You missed a great cooking class. You'll never believe what happened."

She waited for his next message, curious now despite herself.

"Poppy wasn't paying attention like

she should and she nearly burned down her station."

Rissa laughed again, before typing another message.

"WHAT!?! Seriously?" She hit SEND again just as another message came through.

"IDK the whole story behind what went down because I was actually doing what I was supposed to be doing. But something happened and her toaster oven caught fire. The fire alarms and the sprinklers went off and then we were all —"

A moment later, another text appeared.

". . . outside in lines waiting for the fire trucks. She tried to shrug it off, but

she was definitely embarrassed. It was great!"

Rissa laughed again. Wasn't it just her luck that she had to leave school the one time Poppy actually did something that embarrassed her in front of the rest of the school.

The phone vibrated in her hand again, and she looked down at the new message with a smile.

"So, do you need someone to pick up your assignments tomorrow or anything?"

There was a strange fluttering in her stomach that Rissa didn't understand at all when she read Alex's message. She stood there just holding the phone for the longest time trying to decide what it meant and what she should say back to him.

No one ever texted her. . . never. And she didn't want to sound ungrateful or weird, but she had no idea what to say.

"Miss Rissa, is everything all right?" Bernadette's voice distracted her from her internal debate.

"Yes, Bernadette. I'm just fine." A second later, she realized that Bernadette had probably had text conversations with people.

More than I have anyway.

Maybe she would know what to say. Rissa jumped on the chance to ask someone's advice whom she actually trusted to be honest with her. "Bernadette, can I ask your advice about something?"

"Of course, Miss."

"This boy helped me to the nurse's office today when—" She stopped her explanation there, knowing how Bernadette hated hearing about her panic attacks.

"Well, anyway, he just texted me about this thing that happened at school after Mom picked me up and asked if he could bring me homework assignments or anything."

"Oh, how sweet, Miss." She moved closer, as if she were going to look at the phone in Rissa's hand, but backed off before she actually looked at the screen.

Chapter Seven

Rissa solved the problem by handing the phone to her. "I have no idea what to say and he was really nice today. . . and just now. I mean, he didn't have to text me. He didn't have to check in on me. And he didn't have to offer to get my assignments. But he did and I don't know what to say to him."

When Bernadette looked up from the screen a few seconds later, Rissa added, "Help. Please."

"Yes, Miss. Of course." She handed the phone back to Rissa.

"You like this boy, Miss?"

It took Rissa a few seconds to figure out what Bernadette meant. When she did, she wasn't sure how to answer.

"I'm sorry, Miss Rissa. I said the wrong thing."

Rissa rushed in to reassure the young woman. "Not at all, Bernadette. I mean, I do like him. I'm just not really sure if I like him like I think you mean."

"I see, Miss."

"I mean, I think maybe I do." Rissa let out a breath that was much shakier than she expected. "Maybe I don't want to admit that I like him like that because admitting it kind of makes it real, and if he's being a jerk or just messing with me, I don't want to end up getting hurt. Does that make sense?"

Bernadette was nodding her head before Rissa even stopped talking. "Yes, Miss. It makes perfect sense." She patted Rissa's hand. Her voice was full of sadness, as well as something else when she went on.

"You have had such a rough time at that school, Miss. What you say makes all the sense in the world. I have always said you have your head on right, Miss."

"Thank you, Bernadette."

"Of course, Miss."

"Now, what do I say to him?"

"You tell him you look forward to hearing more of the story from him at school tomorrow, of course."

Rissa giggled at the expression on Bernadette's delicate features. "That's perfect!"

For the first time since Rissa could remember, she was actually excited to arrive at school—mostly. A part of her was still kind of freaking out.

She felt kind of like her stomach was doing jumping jacks. She had been so nervous, she hadn't been able to take a bite of breakfast. If her mother had noticed, she hadn't said anything.

Not that her mother ever ate breakfast. She had coffee and sometimes a banana, but mostly she just sat at the table with Rissa and looked at her cell phone.

Her dad, bless him, had noticed. He had commented about how much he enjoyed breakfast, but his voice had been full of concern when he'd said, "Just please tell me you're not going to let those silly kids start dictating your eating habits, sweet pea."

Any other morning, it would have had Rissa stuffing food in her mouth to make sure he knew she was not starving herself.

This morning all she could do was assure him that she was not starving herself as she nibbled at a muffin. She knew better than to tell her dad why she was nervous.

If she told her dad she was meeting a boy before school, he would have insisted on driving her to school and checking the boy out to make sure he was good enough for Rissa—or some such parent nonsense.

If Alex's intentions were less than good and he left her just standing there, she wasn't sure there was a big enough word to describer her embarrassment, not to mention how bad it would make her dad feel to watch his baby girl get stood up at school.

So, she stood in front of the school building by herself—waiting—after having walked in and back out when David, their driver, dropped her off. She did not want to explain to him why she would be waiting outside the school for someone.

After all, he worked for her parents. It just made sense that he would tell her parents about any strange behavior on her part.

"Hi, Rissa." Alex's voice pulled her out of her thoughts.

She let out a very nervous laugh before answering, and when she did, her voice was more than a little shaky. Not really a surprise since inside, she was shouting, *He came. He came! He really came.*

"Hi, Alex. Good morning." Thankfully, she did manage to keep some of the excitement out of her voice.

"How are you today, Rissa? Better, I hope?" There was concern in his voice. She was not just imagining it.

Still. . . Rissa wasn't certain how to take it. The only boy she had really talked to, other than her dad, was David. Most of the people who worked for them were women—even their gardener. Was he just showing concern, like a friend would? Or could it be something more?

"I really am better. Thanks." She shrugged a little, desperate to sound casual, like it was no big deal that she'd almost passed out the day before, with him watching—and possibly freaking out.

"Honestly, I get panic attacks a lot. I am sorry though, that you ended up having to practically drag me to the nurse's office." She could feel the blood rush through her face as she apologized.

What would he think of that? Would he assume she was easily embarrassed?

Will he think I—

She cut that thought off immediately, and even though years of her own feelings of insecurity were weighing heavily on her, she forced herself to be logical.

Just because her mother had thought she was faking the panic attacks, did not mean Alex would.

Come on, Rissa... have a little faith in people.

For some reason it did not help.

"Well, it may be no big deal for you, but it was a totally new thing for me, and I don't mind saying it was pretty scary."

She shrugged again, trying to analyze everything he said—and how he'd said it, to try and figure out what it all meant.

"Anyway, what I told you last night in my text about yesterday, that was pretty much it. I know you said you wanted to hear more about it today, and I mean. . . the whole thing was pretty funny, but there really isn't a whole lot more to it."

He shrugged as he said it, and Rissa watched him as she answered, "Oh. Okay." Would he walk away from her now that he'd said there was nothing left to tell?

He didn't move though. He didn't even turn towards the school building. He just stood there looking at her until the first warning bell rang.

Even then he didn't turn. He stayed where he was, still looking at her. "So, cool if I walk you to class?"

She could only nod.

He turned then, with her. They walked towards the school together and he opened the door for her.

She ducked her head as she walked in ahead of him. If the heat was any indicator, her cheeks must be stained a deep red. It certainly felt like all her blood had relocated to her face.

He didn't seem to notice.

"So, you've heard about this cooking contest, I'm sure. You're going to enter, right?"

She looked up at him. No, she hadn't heard of a cooking contest.

"O. . . K. . . I can see from your face that you have no idea what I'm talking about."

She shook her head.

He smacked a hand to his forehead. "I should have realized. I mean, I heard about it yesterday in class. I just figured. . . ya know. . ." He looked a bit uneasy.

"I mean, Mrs. Peasy likes you so much and she's always going on about your talent. I was sure she would have told you already so you could enter, but maybe she just found out about it or something."

Rissa nodded, but said nothing. She wanted to think that Alex was right, but her history with people did little to convince her of it.

"You are going to enter aren't you?" He sounded concerned all of a sudden, as if he could read the uncertainty on her face.

She wanted to tell him she wasn't

certain if she should. There was such doubt filling her now, and so unexpectedly, it was difficult to even think of what she could possibly cook to compete with others in Silver City.

And then, the words of what had become her favorite song lately came to her. She wanted to make waves. She wanted to fight.

"Yes, I am. I'm going to enter. And I'm going to win."

"Yeah. That, I believe." He grinned.

And somehow she believed it, too.

Chapter Eight

Rissa stopped at the rear entrance, nervous about her parents, about inviting Alex to her house, about entering the contest, and about having to compete with who knew how many other cooks in the city...

She had buzzed Alex in without saying anything to her mom. Then, she'd headed downstairs to meet him—and all the way there she had worried over her agreement.

It had been easy to agree with him earlier that she could win the cooking contest, but almost immediately doubt had seeped in and she'd begun to question the entire conversation.

Could she do this? Would she only end up making a fool of herself? Messing up would just succeed in giving Poppy and her followers one more way to make fun of her.

And her parents. . . she'd said nothing to either of them about the cooking contest or Alex coming over to help her prepare for it.

She had a pretty good idea what her dad's feelings would be about the contest, but her mom's reaction was a mystery—one Rissa was in no hurry to solve.

If she was serious about wanting Rissa to quit her cooking classes, there was also a good chance she would be completely against her entering a city-wide contest.

But there was a chance that Alex's presence would convince her it was a good idea, especially if she mentioned that he was the one who had encouraged Rissa to enter.

What would they think about that? For years they had pressed her to make more friends. Even when she had insisted that she did try, they were never satisfied with her explanation that no one wanted to be friends with her.

And then there was the most pressing worry. They only had a few weeks until the contest and they would have to work super hard between now and then if they hoped to be ready in time.

There would be no time for arguing with her mother about cooking.

She opened the door to see that Alex, much like her, had been dropped off by a driver. He waved as the car drove around the large circle in front of their garage.

"Looks like we have a lot more in common than I thought." She spoke without thinking, but the moment the words were out, she regretted saying anything.

What if he were sensitive about his situation? Would he be thinking that she'd just insulted him? Or would he think that she was flirting with him, trying to make more of something that was actually nothing?

He surprised her when he laughed. "Yeah. Really. Is it as much fun for you?"

She recognized the tone in his voice that described her mood sometimes when she thought about her weird relationship with her parents, especially her mother.

So she answered honestly. "Not even a little bit."

He nodded, then frowned, looking behind him at the car slowly pulled away, then shook his head a little as he turned back to face her. "So, where's your kitchen?"

She smiled, feeling like maybe she'd said exactly the right thing after all. "It's in here." She pushed through the door from the back hall into her favorite room in the house.

He followed, and she was surprised to hear a whistle from behind her.

"Wow. This is some kitchen."

An unexpected warmth filled her. The kitchen was something she had worked on with her father and grandmother. Her mother had only made one suggestion—to make the walls extra thick so sound would not carry into the dining room.

"Our kitchen at home is like, half this. And yours looks like what I've seen in restaurants... fancy restaurants."

He reached up to touch a finger to one of the brass-bottomed pots hanging from a rack attached to the ceiling. "Impressive."

It took her a few seconds to put a reply together in her head that didn't sound silly. "My dad and grandmother helped design it. Grams owns a restaurant downtown."

He started to say something, but stopped, then frowned, and just when she started to ask what was wrong, he said, "Wait, you said Grams? Is that. . .

are you talking about *Grams*? Is that your grandmother's place?"

Rissa began nodding while he was still speaking. His reaction didn't make a lot of sense. Even though she knew it was a nice restaurant, it obviously wasn't as impressive to her as it was to him. To her, it was just a wonderful place to eat with her family every week.

"Wow. I was impressed before, but now. . . I mean. . . Wow." He trailed off, shaking his head as he walked over to lean against a counter. "Your family is seriously cool."

She laughed a little at that. If only he knew the truth about them. . . the enormous group, crammed together around an equally enormous table, tucked away in a room beside the restaurant kitchen, talking over each other, spilling drinks, the little kids tossing the occasional meatball.

"Wait, why is that funny?"

She laughed again before answering. "I was just thinking about our last family dinner. You might not be quite so awed by them after a meal with all of them."

"Oh, I don't know about that."

"Well, then, you'll have to come to the next one, won't you? See which one of us is right."

He opened his mouth, closed it, opened it again, and after a couple of stuttering sounds that were impossible to make out, he finally said, "Are you seriously inviting me to dinner at

Gram's—with your family?"

It was Rissa's turn to panic. What had she said? Was it the wrong thing? Had she insulted him or given him the wrong idea or what?

Just when she was debating whether to run from the room—and keep running—he said, "Hey, take it easy."

She breathed a little easier then.

He went on. "That was awe again, nothing else. I would seriously be honored to have dinner with your family at *Gram's.* Wow. I can hardly say that and actually believe it."

Oh boy. Good. I didn't say the wrong thing.

It occurred to her that she really needed to get better at talking to boys. . .

at people in general, really.

"So, now that we've both had a little freak out, should we get started?" He laughed then, but she was fairly sure it was a nervous laugh—one at their mutual misunderstanding—not one at her or anything she had done.

"Yes. That sounds good."

She turned to the counter and began pulling out cookbooks. This she could do without worrying about something being wrong.

Chapter Nine

Rissa leaned against the wall, looking over the notes she and Alex had made the night before, while she waited for his driver to drop him off in front of the school.

She still wanted to laugh over the irony of the entire situation. She had practically worried herself to death over what her parents would think about Alex being there in the kitchen with her.

When they had walked in—only twenty minutes before Alex was supposed to be picked up—they had been excited. . . ecstatic. . . effusive.

They had insisted he stay for dinner. And all through dinner, they had done nothing but talk about her and her many accomplishments.

Her mother had even made a point to praise her cooking several times during the meal.

Now, in the light of day she could look back and laugh over the ridiculousness of it all. But the evening before, it had only served to embarrass her—and it hadn't helped that Alex had smiled and nodded like he was grateful to them for allowing him in on a family event.

She had sat low in her seat, blushing furiously and barely touching her food, a strange knot forming in her throat.

Now, of course, she could see how silly she had been to be embarrassed. Alex had obviously been playing along with her parents. He already knew she could cook. And, for some reason he felt responsible for her—or sorry for her.

He didn't like her. That couldn't be why he was doing any of this.

Could it?

She wanted to tell herself that was all there was to it.

Of course it was. It had to be.

Suddenly she was nervous again. If he was spending time with her for a reason other than feeling concerned about her, or feeling sorry for her. . . if he actually did like her. . .

Or worse, if he was playing her. . .

If it was like one of those things that happened in the movies, where a popular guy pretends to like an unpopular girl, to win a bet or to set her up for some mean prank.

How would she find out? And if she did find out it was something like that?

She stopped herself, recognizing the warning signs of a panic attack. Her throat was closing up. Her breaths were coming harder, faster, and shallow. Her chest felt tight.

"Hi, Rissa."

It was all she could do not to turn and run, as far and as fast as her legs would carry her.

She could find a phone and call her dad. He would send their driver to pick her up. She—

"What happened?"

His question distracted her just enough, and had her wondering how he always seemed to be able to read her face so easily.

"Come on, Rissa. I know that look. Something happened. Was it Poppy? Has she already been here and been causing trouble? Are you all right?"

He reached out and squeezed her shoulder gently, confusing her even further.

What was she to think? Every bit of the experience she had with kids her age told her that there was something going on. . . that he was not merely being nice to her.

Either he wanted something—or he was up to something.

But his own words, his actions, and his mysterious ability to read her face, her breathing, her posture, told her he was genuine. . . that he was a friend, a confidant, someone she could depend on.

"Rissa, would you please say

something? You're really starting to scare me." A moment later, he added, "If it's not Poppy, what is it? Was it your parents? Did they freak out last night after I left? Did they give you a hard time?"

Another gentle squeeze, only this time it was both shoulders.

"Please, talk to me. Tell me what's wrong."

She opened her mouth to speak, determined to be cool about the whole thing, but then her words got away from her. "Is it a bet or something, or a plot? Was it all Poppy's idea? What's the end game here? Are you planning to embarrass me at the contest, in front of the whole city? Is that it? Why me? What did I do to anyone? Seriously... I do not understand." The whole thing came out in a crazed jumble and the last few words were impossible to understand because she was crying, tears streaming down her cheeks.

He did the last thing she expected. He pulled her against him, wrapping her in a warm hug, gently leading her around the corner and away from the students who were suddenly very interested in what was going on with the least popular girl at school.

It was several minutes before she calmed down enough to pull away. When she did, Alex put a hand on each shoulder and leaned down enough that he could look into her eyes.

"I understand if you would rather I not come by your house after school today. We don't have to sit together at lunch. And I promise you, I am not angry or upset."

There was a strange feeling in her chest, an unfamiliar emotion she wasn't sure she wanted to examine closely.

Could he be telling the truth?

Was it really possible that one of the most popular boys in school was hanging around with her because he truly enjoyed her company?

"I don't think I will ever really understand what you've been through in your life, but I want you to know that I have been spending time with you because I want to. There's no plot or bet, nothing nefarious going on, I promise." He let go then, stepped back a little.

"I don't really expect you to believe me. The other idiots we go to school with have pretty much made that impossible for you, haven't they?"

"I want you to sit with me at lunch." She couldn't explain it, but she believed him. She looked up just in time to see him smile.

"And, if you don't come by the house this afternoon, Mom will be very disappointed. I'm not taking that bullet for you." She was surprised at the teasing tone that had crept into her voice.

Was she really teasing him, after she'd nearly had a nervous breakdown and then blubbered all over him?

And still he was smiling. "It's a fair point. She would be pretty bummed, huh?"

Rissa nodded, a smile spreading across her own face. "Yes, she has big plans for dinner. You said you enjoyed last night's meal. Well, she's going to expect you to stay tonight, too.

"All right, we'd better not disappoint her then."

"Right."

When the warning bell rang overhead, he laughed and slung an arm around her shoulders. "Come on. We're gonna be late to class."

Chapter Ten

Somehow she got through the day. Even Poppy and her little group of friends surprised her. Not once did any of them make a nasty or rude comment.

Nothing.

It was almost weird for Rissa. It felt almost like she was waiting for the other shoe to drop.

No one had mentioned her little scene this morning, either. . . and she knew there had been at least a dozen students out front who had seen her break down.

But no one was talking about it. No one was talking about her. All day, the only thing she noticed from the students around her was a complete and utter lack of meanness.

And when David pulled up in front of the school, Alex was right there beside her.

"Mom said to just ride home with you. I'll call when you're sick of me and

Brent will come pick me up." He grinned.

Rissa nearly gasped, panic shooting through her at the realization that her freak out this morning had nearly left him without a way home.

Alex held the door open for her while she climbed into the back seat, climbing in after her and then leaning forward to offer a hand to David.

He looked into the rearview mirror at Rissa, his expression odd, and difficult to decipher, but he accepted Alex's hand and gave it a shake.

"Good to meet you, young man. I've heard a lot about you from Rissa."

"As you say, sir."

Rissa sat quietly, still feeling a little

weird about her morning outburst and Alex's easy acceptance of her damaged perception of the world around her.

Alex chattered almost nonstop, about school, about the upcoming contest, and about some sporting event that he'd watched after getting home the night before. Apparently, that was just the thing to loosen David's tongue.

Suddenly, they were the best of friends. They talked the rest of the way to Rissa's house about sports, several different ones—arguing a little over different teams, averages, records, and a host of other words she had no recognition or understanding of.

When they pulled into the driveway, she knew Alex had won over David, just like he'd won over her parents.

If. . . and she'd accepted it was unlikely at this point, but if he was up to something, he would break more hearts than just hers.

Her mother was waiting for them in the back hallway, a box from the local bakery resting on her open palms.

"Oh, good. You're right on time." She gave Rissa an odd look, but reached up to open the lid on the box, holding it out to the two of them. "Pastry?"

Alex didn't even hesitate, picking up a

large bear claw and taking a bite, muttering something that sounded like "Mmm. This is great."

Rissa saw her mom smile and couldn't help but shake her head at the irony of the situation. Her mother—who was constantly on a diet, who never ate sweets, who would barely even allow them in the house—was standing there offering them sweets as if it was a normal after school snack.

When her mother kept the lid open, Rissa reached in and selected an apple fritter. They weren't as good as the recipe her Grams had shared with her, but they weren't half bad, and they had a lot of work ahead of them.

Last night she and Alex had gone

through the cookbooks until they found five recipes to make. Her parents had agreed at dinner to be her guinea pigs, so the five recipes would be their dinner tonight.

Now they needed to get cooking—and since apple fritters were not on the menu, Rissa was determined to enjoy this one. Plus, she knew the sugar boost would come in handy.

"Thanks, Mom."

"Oh, it's my pleasure, sweetie." She dropped the box lid and put an arm around Rissa's shoulders as they moved slowly toward the kitchen. "Anything for my girl."

Rissa nodded, but said nothing. She could feel the urge to scoff at her mother's words, but didn't want to take a chance on embarrassing her.

"So, Alex, I guess we should get started."

Her mom was not so quick to take the hint. She followed them into the kitchen, setting the large bakery box on the counter right inside the door.

"So, you're going to make five different recipes for us to taste tonight?"

"Yes, Mom. We need to know which one tastes best, looks best, and is easiest to handle when eating small test bites." She explained again, with only a little huff in her voice.

Fortunately, her mother was oblivious. She stood beside the counter, watching Rissa... and Alex, as he moved around the kitchen picking up ingredients and utensils.

Rissa watched, marveling at how quickly he had learned where everything was in the kitchen.

He walked around like he'd been prepping and cooking in this kitchen for years, the way she had.

Finally, her mom got the idea.

"Well, I'll just get out of your way. I wouldn't want to distract you or anything."

Rissa rolled her eyes a little, but said nothing, returning the quick hug her mother gave her as she passed.

"We'll be ready by dinner time."

"Sounds great." And with a little wave, she was gone.

Rissa let out a little breath and turned to look at Alex, who was grinning as widely as his face would allow.

"You handled that well."

She laughed. He was forever reading her emotions—and, though her mother didn't seem to have picked up on her irritation, he clearly had.

"Okay. Okay. Make fun of me later. Right now, let's get cooking."

He laughed as she swatted playfully at him with a spatula.

Chapter Eleven

The morning of the contest the weather was nearly perfect. The sky was a clear, cloudless, stretch of blue. Traffic was much better than Rissa expected.

She arrived at the convention center

early, checked in, got her station number and paperwork in record time.

Alex was there waiting for her. He helped David unload the van they had brought, the one her dad had borrowed from his mother.

It was a large, white van she used for picking things up for her restaurant, and occasionally for deliveries. Since they rarely ever used it, it didn't have the restaurant name stenciled on the side like the regular delivery van, for which Rissa was oddly grateful.

If everyone saw the name *Gram's* on the van as they unloaded, they would expect more from her before she even got started.

Thankfully, the good Lord knew she

didn't need any more pressure than she had on her already.

With Alex's help, the van was unloaded in minutes. She didn't even get to help. Every time she reached for something, Alex or David took it out of her hands.

They stacked everything on two hand carts, and pulled them into the building. All she could do was follow behind them.

They did the same with the unloading at her station. She picked up several things, only to have one of the two take it from her and set it down in the miniature kitchen that would be hers for the duration of the contest.

A few minutes later, David took the two hand carts and left to move the van.

Alex stayed behind and started moving and re-stacking boxes and bags of supplies.

Rissa busied herself with putting on the apron that matched the ones that had been provided for each contestant and their assistant.

All around them, other teams were doing exactly what they were doing, unloading supplies and putting on aprons.

No one was allowed to do more than arrange their supplies before the contest officially began. They could unpack bowls, utensils, and individual packages of ingredients, but they were not allowed to open anything or put it into the bowls or measuring cups or spoons.

Everyone would have the exact same amount of time to prep and cook, and while Rissa knew she would be a bundle of nerves long before the starting bell was rung, she told herself there would be other people in the same position.

"Rissa." Alex's voice interrupted her. "I can see you starting to freak out. Relax."

She shook her head, but he went on. "You're not fooling me. You're stressing. Stop." He moved around until he was standing right in front of her. He took both her hands in his and squeezed gently. "You've got this. You know you do."

She nodded again, but he kept talking. "I will be right here next to you the whole time. Just breathe."

When she laughed, he did, too. "You are gonna whoop everybody in this room."

They both laughed and somehow the tension melted away.

"Hey, let's go grab a snack. We have time."

She nodded again, even though she knew her throat was way too tight to let food through. At least she could get a drink.

She followed Alex across the room and avoided looking at the stations they passes, knowing it would only make her nervous again.

All the way on the far side of the room, there were several tables set up with finger foods and small sandwiches.

They had coffee, soft drinks, bottled water, and hot water for tea or cocoa. She followed Alex as he grabbed a plate and started filling it up.

She nearly laughed when he reached the end of the table, and his plate was piled high. It was not surprising at all that he'd picked up so much. When she looked around at the men—and a few boys—who were standing around or sitting nearby, holding their own plates, they were all piled just as high as his.

"Are you sure you don't want anything?"

She smiled at him, shaking her head, even while she held back a desire to laugh.

"What?" His voice held a playful sound of shock?

"I didn't say anything."

"But you were thinking it."

She shook her head. Would he never stop reading her face?

"I'm going to go get a drink. You want something?" He slid his plate onto a tall, round table beside them and went back to the snack tables to choose a drink.

When he returned, he handed her a bottle of water. "At least hydrate."

She laughed and took the bottle from him, twisting off the top and taking a small drink as she looked around.

These people were her competition. They were the ones who would be working hard to outdo her.

No one was making fun of her. No one was looking at her, talking behind their hands, pointing and laughing. No one looked at her with anything more than the same scrutiny she was giving them.

They were only judging her on her ability to win the contest.

I can't wait to be part of the adult world, where people don't make fun of others to be mean, or just because they can.

The realization that these would be the sort of people she would spend her career surrounded by made her feel better about the cooking contest, and that Alex had convinced her to enter.

Nearly twenty minutes later, when Alex had emptied his plate, and she'd emptied her water bottle and started on another, they headed back toward their station.

They spent the next half hour setting up as much as they could, opening boxes, setting out utensils and bowls, arranging ingredients in the order they would need them and in a way that would be easy to grab when needed.

Alex tied on his apron and Rissa slipped away to the bathroom. When she was done, she retied her hair, doing everything she could to be sure it was secure and would not come loose while they were working.

She looked at herself in the mirror, full cheeks, rounded shoulders, wide hips, short stature, no jewelry, a basic clip in her hair, and a face entirely devoid of makeup.

She was surprised to realize she liked what she saw in front of her. Several weeks ago, she would have glanced in the mirror and looked quickly away, unhappy with herself because many of her classmates told her she should be.

But now, knowing that the people in the room she was about to enter were only going to judge her on her work and her talent with food, she was surprised to realize the reflection staring back at her was actually pretty.

Her smile lit up her face in a way it probably never had before, and the excitement that was starting to flow through her veins gave her skin a healthy glow that most people used powders and liquids to simulate.

"I can do this." She told her reflection. Then, she laughed a little at how silly she felt, talking to herself.

And with a deep breath, she squared her shoulders and turned to push her way out of the room, feeling certain that she was going to win this contest.

Chapter Twelve

Poppy surprised Rissa the next afternoon at school.

In front of everyone in the cafeteria, she walked over to where Rissa sat, and took the chair across the table from her.

Then, before Rissa could think of anything to say, she spoke. "That was really cool, you winning the contest and all."

Rissa opened her mouth, but hadn't a clue what she should say. Before she could utter even a single sound, Poppy went on.

"I mean. . . winning the whole thing, against adults and cooks who have trained in actual restaurant kitchens. . . I'm just saying wow. It was really cool."

Rissa opened her mouth again to speak, but Poppy was already standing up.

"See ya around, girl." Then she was gone, walking across the cafeteria to sit at her usual table.

"Was that Poppy…sitting here?"

Rissa nodded, but couldn't seem to get any actual words out.

"Are you all right?"

Rissa nodded again.

"What did she want?" Alex sat down across from her, in the seat Poppy had just vacated—and Rissa finally found her voice.

"She wanted to tell me how cool it was, that I won yesterday." She looked across the room, at where Poppy sat, holding court like she always did, with her friends all around her.

Was it really possible that Poppy had actually sat down across from her, and more or less congratulated her on a big exciting win?

It felt like it couldn't possible be real.

"Well, you know what they say. . ." When he said nothing else, Rissa turned back to look at Alex.

"No, what do they say?"

"This could be the beginning of a beautiful friendship."

Rissa laughed for a full minute.

This is NOT the end...

It's just the beginning!

"For God hath not given us the spirit of fear; but of power, and love, and of a sound mind."
~ II Timothy 1:7

A NOTE FROM MACY

Magic, wondrous characters, and fantastical stories are only a few of the things I love about Fairy Tales.

And, as much as I love the originals, I love making new stories for the beloved characters we've all grown up with.

I hope readers who enjoy Fairy Tales as much as I do, will enjoy the modern twists my mother and I have added to these much-loved stories.

~ Macy

"For God so loved the world, that He gave His only begotten Son, that whosoever believeth in Him should not perish, but have everlasting life."
~ John 3:16

A NOTE FROM JC

This story has a special signifigance to me, and had a powerful impact on me while working on it.

I went through school with children from all sides making fun of me for the way I dressed, because I tended to be more rambunctious than the other girls, and due to the fact that I was happier with my nose in a book than a fashion magazine.

And yes, I was picked on over my size... mercilessly—and it is deliberately ironic that, while I was not one bit overweight in school, it has been a constant struggle ever since.

We desperately need to end body shaming and teach our children it is better to be healthy than it is to be thin!

~ JC

"Call unto me, and I will answer thee,
and shew thee great and mighty things,
which thou knowest not."
~ Jeremiah 33:3

ABOUT THE AUTHORS

Macy Morrows is a young girl following in her mother's footsteps, with storytelling, having her head in the clouds, and spending her time in fictional worlds. She fits in better than her mother ever did though. . . and that's not a bad thing.

JC Morrows is an author of fantastical fiction filled with faith. She writes about assassins, aliens, dragons, angels, fairy tales, and teenagers trying desperately to survive in post-apocalptic worlds.

She also drinks coffee. . . lots and lots of coffee.

DON'T MISS BOOK ONE

WELCOME TO SILVER CITY: WHERE HAPPILY EVER AFTER IS STILL A MODERN GIRL'S DREAM!

Meet Cindy, a soft-spoken maid-in-training who secretly wishes she could do a little more than clean the prince's toilets...

As good as orphaned, Cindy works for her step-mother, who owns a high class maid service that caters to the well-to-do families of Silver City.

BOOK ONE OF THE SILVER CITY PRINCESS STORIES

MORE FROM JC & MACY

As if being a teenager isn't hard enough. . .

Can you imagine how it feels to wake up one day and find out that you are not who you thought you were?

If you're anything like me, you know it's hard enough trying to fit in—in high school—without having to deal with the knowledge that your dad is an alien part of the time. I don't even get how you can be an alien part of the time. . .

As if I don't have enough to deal with. . .

It's crazy enough to find out, the hard way, that you are not who you thought you were.

But to have that kind of bombshell dropped on you, and then — to have your Dad ditch you — leaving you to figure stuff out all by yourself, with a Mom you can't tell anything about what's going on. . . and school enemies lurking around unexpected corners.

MORE FROM S&G Publishing

SOPHIE IS A KITTEN WHO FOUND TWO CHILDREN . . . AND DECIDED TO ADOPT THEM AS HER OWN

Read along with Sammy and Macy as they tell the story of finding a little lost kitten, naming her, loving her, and making her part of their (or rather, becoming her own) family.

Enjoy Thanksgiving with them. Read about how Sophie celebrates this fun holiday filled with food, family and mischief.

Then read about how Sophie's family made the move from the big city... and Sophie followed.

Now she has her own house, a big yard, and new kitty friends right next door!

Katie Chupp spends her days at The Sweet Shop, taking care of customers and baking delicious treats... not exactly a profession where one expects to be thrown into the midst of mysteries and mayhem.

But when the bakery is broken into, someone has to find the thief . . . besides finding another place to do the baking and get the orders to the customers.

Is this a random theft, or is the thief trying to ruin the town's Independence Day celebration?

It's the most wonderful time of the year and Katie Chupp is spending her days catering to the holiday rush. With everyone in town ordering special desserts and treats, will Katie be able to find time to finish making gifts for her family and friends?

With a winter chill settling in and Christmas right around the corner, no one would expect a mystery, but a mystery does indeed appear... And this is one mystery that may never be solved...

Amelia Simpkins may be a great cook, and have a head for business, but sweet treats are out of her league and the owner of the Irish Blessings Cafe says it's because she adds the tart to the Sweet Shop's new dessert that Katie Chupp insists is only filled with lemony goodness.

The two shop owners' constant bickering sends sparks flying through Abbott Creek's usual calm... and when Andrew's cafe suffers from some rather unusual pest problems, the town starts taking sides.

It's the time of year when the residents of Abbott Creek give thanks for their blessings.

But Katie is having difficulty deciding whether she should be thankful. . . or careful of the new relationships she has developed over the previous year...

Katie Chupp is not the only person in Abbott Creek looking forward to the most romantic holiday of the year...

But Valentine's Day will not be all hearts and flowers. There are secrets to be kept, feelings to be explored, and difficult decisions to be made — and each one has something to do with the heart.

Will those secrets come between friends? Will the happy couples in Abbott Creek get to celebrate. . . together?

Between babies and budding romances, busy schedules and unexpected gossip, the small town and its residents may never be the same.

Everyone at the Sweet Shop Bakery and the Irish Blessings cafe is worrying over Bella and her baby – and busily trying to convince her to take it easy.

Katie is not the only person in town with some big decisions ahead of her. And the busy summer season is kicked off with a big surprise for everyone.

9 781948 733496